For
Ma and Pa
with very much love

and, with grateful thanks,
to
the Walker "Moles" team
for their patience.
C.A.

First published 1994 by
Walker Books Ltd
87 Vauxhall Walk, London SE11 5HJ

This edition published 1995

2 4 6 8 10 9 7 5 3 1

Text © 1994 Richard Edwards
Illustrations © 1994 Caroline Anstey

This book has been typeset in Monotype Garamond.

Printed in Hong Kong

British Library Cataloguing in Publication Data
A catalogue record for this book is available
from the British Library.

ISBN 0-7445-4310-X

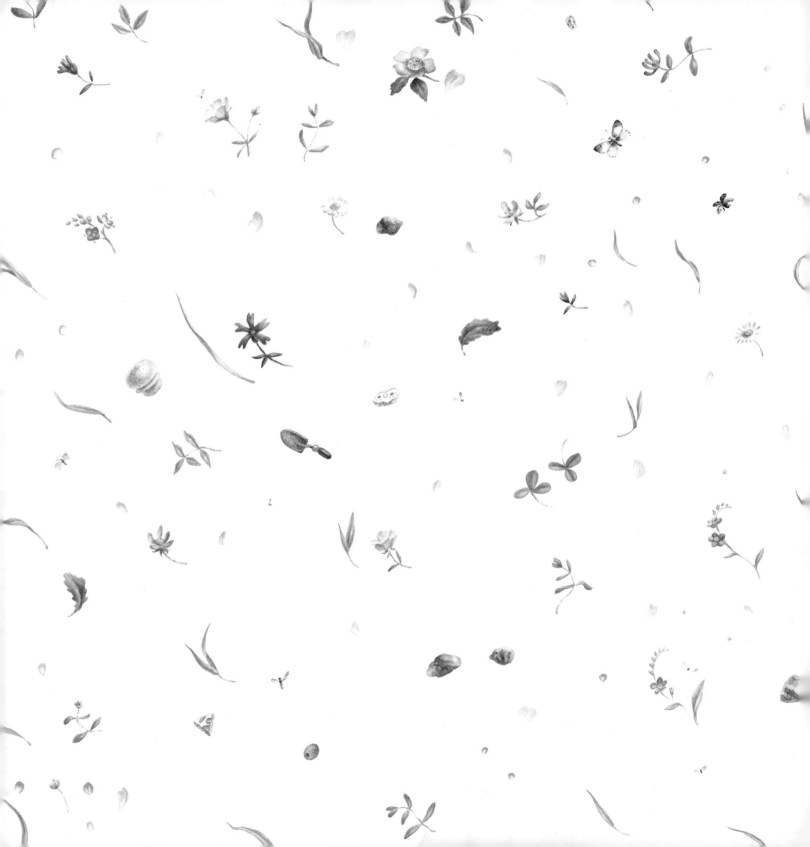

MOLES CAN DANCE

Written by Richard Edwards

Illustrated by Caroline Anstey

Walker Books
AND SUBSIDIARIES
LONDON · BOSTON · SYDNEY

In the
warm wormy darkness
underground, moles were doing
their work. All day long they dug
tunnels and corridors and pushed up
mole-hills into the field above. It was
tiring work and the young mole soon
got bored. "I'm worn out," he said,
"and I'm all cramped up. I don't
like digging. I want to stretch.
I want to run about.
I want to …

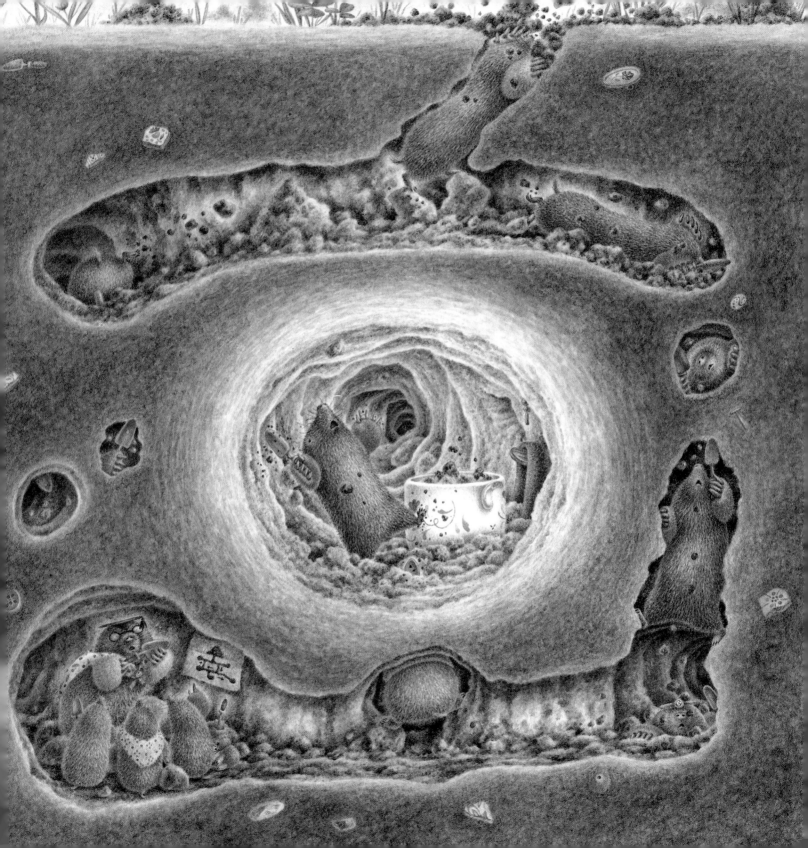

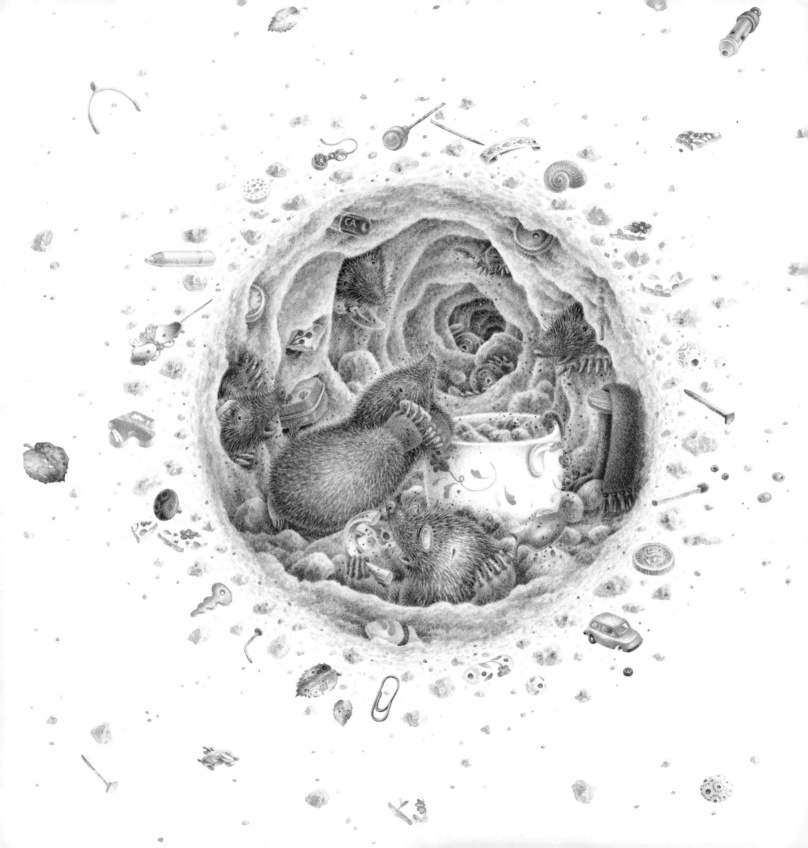

... *dance*!"

"Moles can't dance," said the old mole. "Moles aren't made for dancing, they're made for digging. Whoever heard of a mole dancing!"

"Moles can't dance," said all the other moles.

"See," said the old mole. "What did I tell you? Now stop being silly and dig that tunnel."

The young mole dug as he was told, but all the time he was thinking: I want to learn to dance. Why shouldn't I learn to dance? It's not fair.

Then he had an idea. If the moles couldn't teach him to dance, perhaps someone else could. Quickly he scrabbled his way upwards and broke out into the dazzling sunshine of the field.

A cow was looking at him.

"I want to learn to dance," said the young mole.

"I can't teach you," said the cow. "Cows can't dance. They can chew grass and wave their tails and moo, but they can't dance."

And it went on chewing grass.

The mole walked on and met a frog.
"I want to learn to dance," said the mole.
"I can't teach you," said the frog. "Frogs
can't dance. They can hop about and
swim, but they can't dance."
And it hopped into the
pond and swam away.

Next the mole met a fox.

"I want to learn to dance," said the mole.

"I can't teach you," said the fox. "Foxes can't dance. They can prowl round the fields, keeping very quiet, but they can't dance."

And it went on prowling.

The mole walked on and saw a woodpecker
hammering at a tree.

"I want to learn to dance," called the mole.

"I can't teach you," said the woodpecker.
"Woodpeckers can't dance. They can fly from
tree to tree, bashing the bark with their beaks,
but they can't dance."

And it went on bashing.

Then the mole heard a funny noise coming from behind a hedge.

THUMPA THUMPA THUMPA

What could it be?

THUMPA THUMPA THUMPA

The mole crawled into the hedge and looked out on the other side. Two children were playing in a garden. Dodge was making the THUMPA THUMPA THUMPA by banging on some boxes, and Daisy was dancing on the grass. Real dancing!

The mole had never seen anything so fine in all his life.

Dodge drummed  and Daisy
danced
and the mole watched carefully.

Daisy spun round on one leg
and the mole spun round on one leg.

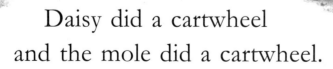

Daisy did a cartwheel
and the mole did a cartwheel.
Daisy hopped up and down and so did the mole.

Every step that Daisy danced,
the mole danced too, until shadows
began to creep across the garden.
"Better get back," said the mole to himself. "It's
getting late." And he turned and began
to dance his way home.

The woodpecker was
so surprised to see the mole
dancing back along the path
that it almost fell off its branch.

The fox was so surprised
to see the mole dancing
along the hedgerow
that it almost
toppled into
a ditch.

The frog was so
surprised to see the mole dancing
past the pond that it swallowed
a mouthful of muddy water.

The cow was so
surprised to see the
mole dancing across
the field that it
stood still for a long
time, with a grass
stalk sticking out
of its mouth.

"Where have you been?" asked the old mole.

"Just … dancing," said the young mole.

"Moles can't dance," said the old mole.

"Oh, yes they can," said the young mole.
"I'll show you." And he climbed on to the top of the
nearest mole-hill and began to hop and spin about.

Soon all the other moles came up to see
what was happening.

"He's dancing!" said one mole.
"And if he can, so can we.

Come on!"

So, in ones and twos and
threes, they all began to dance.
Some on mole-hills, some on the
grass, some very badly, some very well,
some moles hopping, some moles jumping

and some moles spinning
around, but all of them, even
the old mole, having a fine time as
they danced and danced and danced and
danced by the light of the climbing moon.

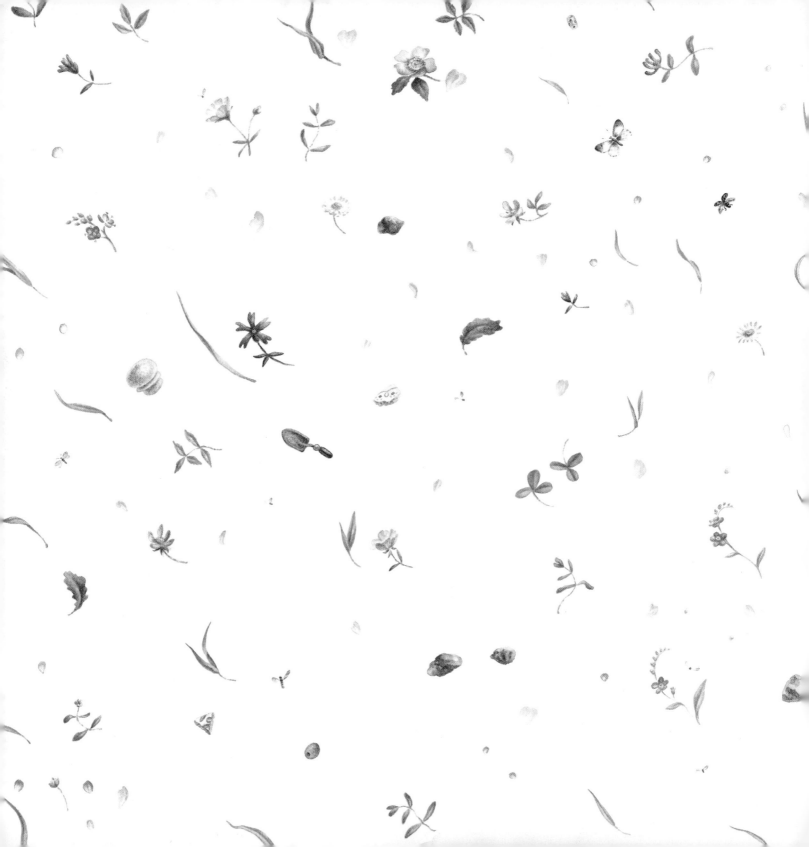

MORE WALKER PAPERBACKS
For You to Enjoy

I BOUGHT MY LOVE A TABBY CAT
by Colin West / Caroline Anstey

"A nonsense rhyme that compares with Edward Lear at his best.
Its fitting and very funny illustrations make it ideal for under fives."
Tony Bradman, Parents

0-7445-2348-6   £3.99

THE CATS OF TIFFANY STREET
by Sarah Hayes

Every Friday night, six cats meet and dance at the end of Tiffany Street.
Then along comes the man with a van and takes them away.

"Admirably suited to reading aloud … will give great pleasure.
The pictures are bold, colourful and full of movement and witty detail. The story is a good one too."
The Times Educational Supplement

0-7445-3162-4   £3.99

FLY BY NIGHT
by June Crebbin / Stephen Lambert

All day long Blink, the young owl, sits on his branch, waiting
impatiently to take flight for the very first time. Will the moment ever arrive?

"A rich introduction to what a good story is all about – perfect
for reading aloud and relishing the pictures." *Children's Books of the Year*

0-7445-3627-8   £3.99

Walker Paperbacks are available from most booksellers, or by post from B.B.C.S., P.O. Box 941, Hull, North Humberside HU1 3YQ

24 hour telephone credit card line 01482 224626

To order, send: Title, author, ISBN number and price for each book ordered, your full name and address, cheque or postal order
payable to BBCS for the total amount and allow the following for postage and packing:
UK and BFPO: £1.00 for the first book, and 50p for each additional book to a maximum of £3.50. Overseas and Eire: £2.00 for the first book, £1.00 for the second and 50p for each additional book.

Prices and availability are subject to change without notice.